D1147958

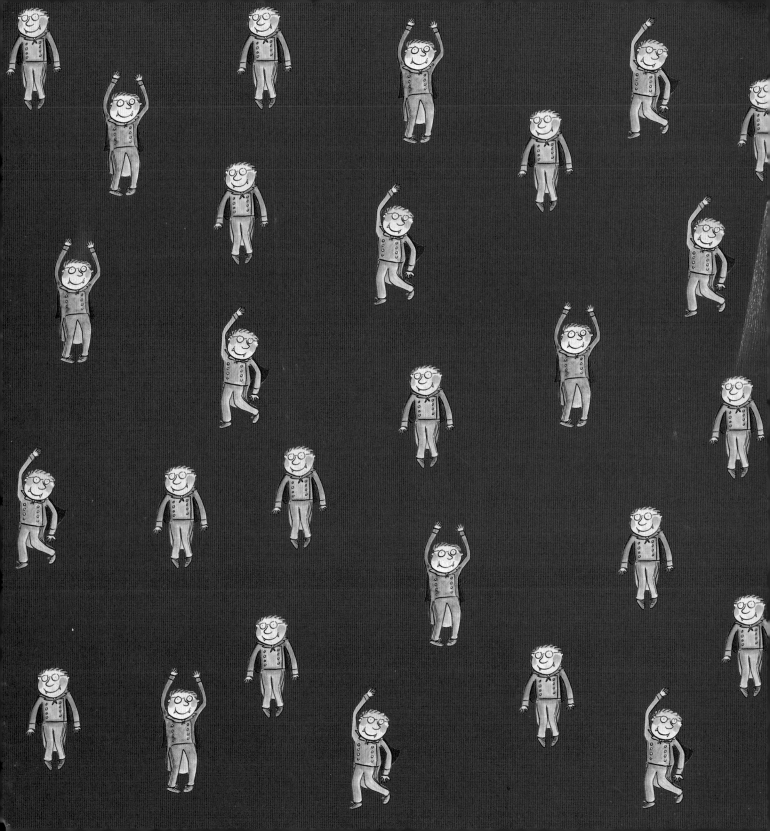

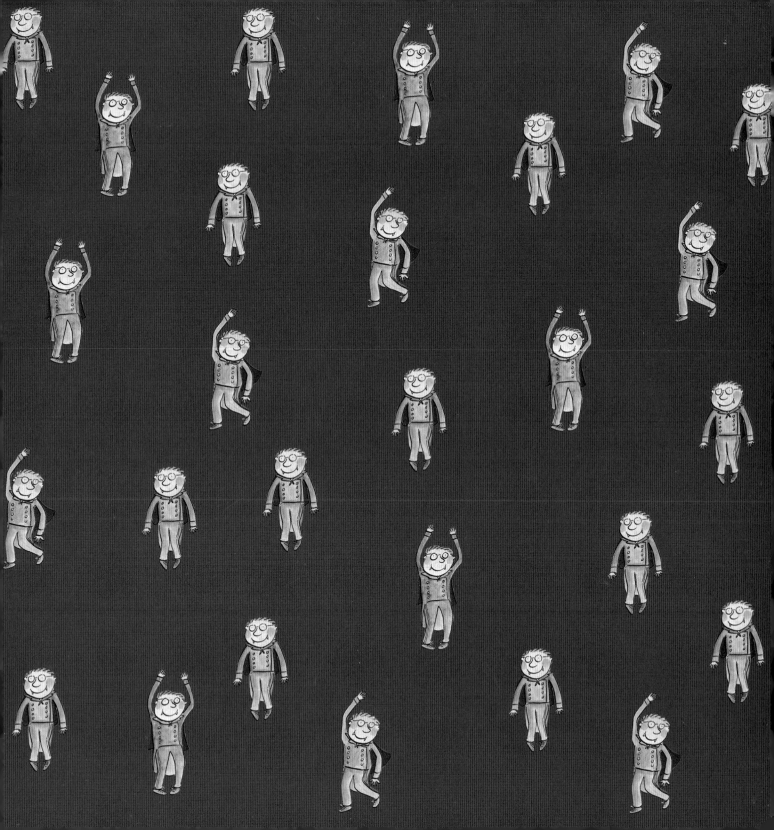

First published in 2016 by © Rockpool Children's
Books Ltd.

This edition published in 2016 by Rockpool Children's
Books Ltd. in association with Albury Books.
Albury Court, Albury, Thame
OX9 2LP, United Kingdom

For orders: Kuperard Publishers and Distributors
+44 (0) 208 4462440

Text copyright © Rosie Brooks 2016
Illustrations copyright © Rosie Brooks 2016

The rights of Rosie Brooks to be identified as
the author and illustrator have been asserted by them
in accordance with the
Copyright, Designs and Patents Act, 1988

A CIP catalogue record of this book is
available from the British Library.
All rights reserved

Printed and bound in China

ISBN 978-1-906081-32-4
(Paperback)

rockpool
children's books

Albury Books

ROSIE BROOKS

VINCE THE VAMPIRE
very nice

Once upon a time there was
a young vampire called Vince...

...who in many ways was
just like other vampires.
He had a cloak,
and he had
a lovely pair of fangs,
but...

...something about Vince was different!

He liked cooking and garlic...

...vegetables, "Yummy!"...

...karaoke...

...busking...

...knitting...

...and horror of horrors... sun bathing!

Yes, Vince was very different!!

Sometimes Vince would try to
hide how different
he was...

...and do vampirey things
with other vampires...

...but Vince wasn't fooling anyone!

The truth was, by vampire
standards, Vince was just TOO NICE!

But, not only was Vince far too
lovely to be scary...

...Vince was very easily
scared himself!

For example, he was scared
of...

Bats, rats, dogs, cats,
spiders, wasps, monsters,
ghosts and ghoulies,
creepy crawlies, venus fly traps,
heights, birds, flying,
snakes, zombies, witches,
thunderstorms, worms,
blood...

...and to cap it all, Vince
was scared of the dark!

However, it didn't stop
Vince having lots of
unsuspecting friends, and one day
they invited him on a camping trip.

He excitedly packed his camping trip essentials...

Oh oh, Trouble!

...and off they went...

...(unfortunately for Vince) into the dark, dark woods!

In the dark, dark woods,
his friends began to play
dark, dark woodsy type games,
and told dark, dark woodsy
type stories...

...and Vince pretended not to be scared,
but in fact, he was terrified!

Then suddenly, just as he thought things couldn't get worse, from through the trees came a blood curdling...

"Ooh, err!" said the gang.
Vince wasn't the only one
scared now!

They tried to howl back
even louder and scarier, but...

This needed action, and in a flash,
Vince did just that,
and flashed his torch into the
dark, dark, trees and said...

.... would you like some of our sweets?

Something ghastly,
ghoulish and ghostly,
began to take shape..

...then out of the trees, bounded
something hideously horrible,
it was Valerie vampire, Vinces sister,
who said...

"I thought you'd
never ask!"

...and they all tucked into
a wonderful midnight feast!

Vince had saved the day
(even though it was just his sist
by being Vince, the very nice Vamp

"da daaaa!"

The End.

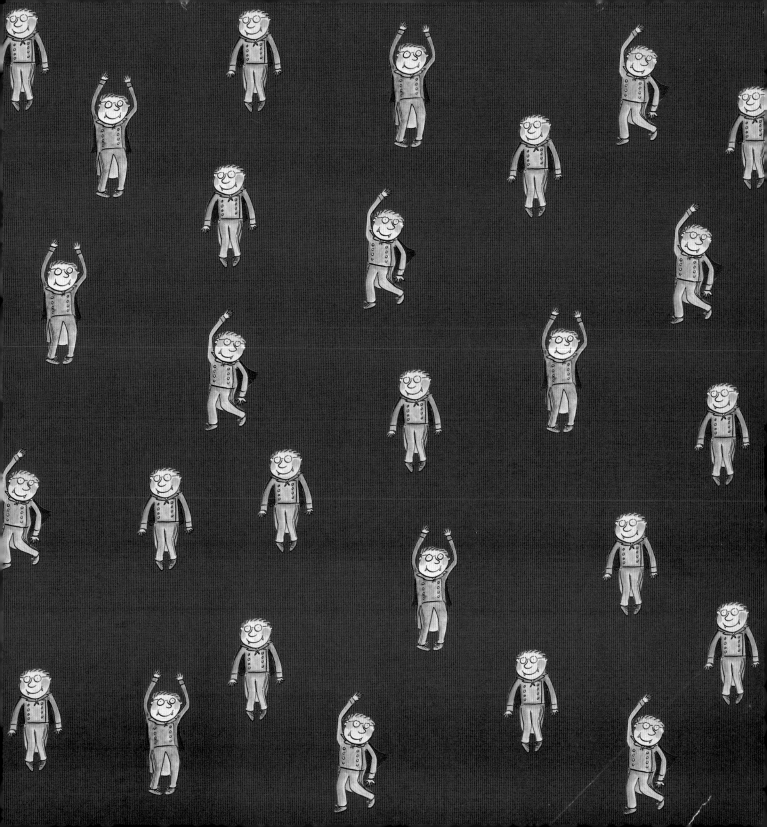

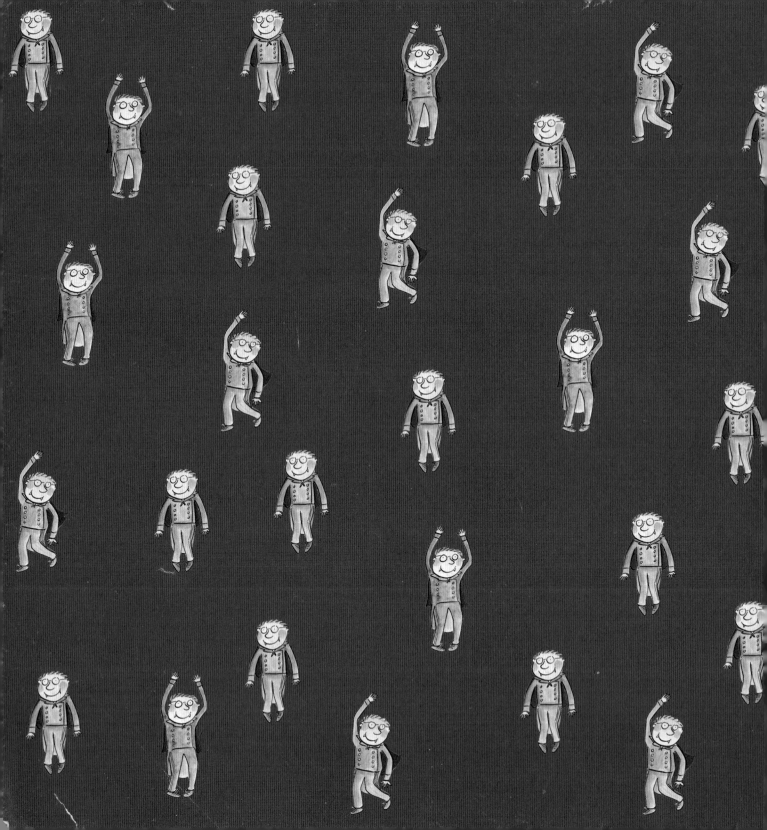